# THE TUNNEL AND OTHER SPECULATIVE FICTION

Raihan Kibria

# CONTENTS

# THE TUNNEL



There was a sound like a huge, viscous bubble bursting, and Mason fell upwards into a hole in space. He'd been in the evening rush-hour crowd, trudging drowsily through the pedestrian subway to his metro station after a long workday. His stomach lurched as he was pulled towards the ceiling, and he went "oof!" when he slammed into a flat surface in sudden, complete darkness. Groaning with pain, he sat up and turned on his smartphone's flashlight. He seemed to be in the same place, but where did everyone go? The familiar dusty green tiles of the tunnel's walls glinted a few meters away. When he shone the light down its length, he could see no end, and no people. There should have been a right turn a little ahead. He turned around, expecting to see the stairs up, but they weren't there either. There was only the straight tunnel. The overhead fluorescent lights were off. It was absolutely silent here; there was no rumbling of distant traffic, or even the slight hum of electrical equipment.

Mason started walking, shouting "Hello!" Nobody answered. Crossing the tunnel should have taken two minutes, but after ten minutes, he was still in the same straight passage. Deciding to try his luck the other way, he doubled back. Twenty minutes later, there was still nothing but a straight, unbranched tunnel. He checked his phone: no signal. What was going on? Was he asleep? He tried to wake himself up by yelling and punching the walls. It gave him only a stinging pain and bruised knuckles.

With no alternative, he traveled onward. Even after two hours at a brisk pace, he was still breathing in the stale, cool air of the straight tunnel. His lunch had been hours ago, and he was growing hungry and thirsty. He checked his briefcase for a candy bar he might have forgotten about, but there were only some pens, a legal pad, and a power bank for the phone. After a few more hours, he lost his composure. He raged, then cried, then collapsed morosely against the wall. In a stupor, he got up and marched until he was too tired. He slept on the tiled floor, using his briefcase as a pillow, and continued on the next morning. He found nothing but the same straight tunnel. After a few days, the dehydration made him first strangely euphoric, then delirious, and eventually it killed him.

## *ITERATION*

Mason was walking through the tunnel with the other commuters when there was a sound like a huge, viscous bubble bursting, and he fell into an empty and seemingly endless version of the same subway. His flashlight revealed a figure sitting beside a rough hole in the wall. Close up, he realized the man looked exactly like him. He was dead, his emaciated body starting to mummify in the cool, dry air. The shoulder-wide hole went up at a forty-five degree angle and ended in dry, brown earth after about five meters.

A legal pad lay beside the dead man. With trembling fingers, he picked it up and saw his own handwriting on it: 'There's no way out. We are trying to dig up to the surface. Cut pieces off of me to eat and survive longer. The eyes are easy and full of water.' Mason stood up, dazed. He saw dozens of dirty metal pens with worn tips on the floor. He had the same one in his briefcase. They'd been used as makeshift pickaxes. Bloodstained shanks made from keys (his apartment keys, he realized) lay nearby. Copies of his phone and his briefcase were strewn all around the dirt-covered floor. There was something else in the distance. It turned out to be more identical corpses, shriveled as ancient mummies. Hundreds of them lined the walls of the passageway. Some had been mutilated, with bits of meat cut out of their legs and buttocks. Many were eyeless, their sockets empty holes. Mason started sobbing and cried out for his mother.

## INTROSPECTION

Mason was walking through the tunnel with the other commuters when there was a sound like a huge, viscous bubble bursting, and gravity suddenly reversed. He dropped onto a pile of something soft. It felt, and smelled, like an old sofa that something had rotted on. Gagging and retching, he turned on his flashlight. He saw in the glare of the blueish beam that he was surrounded by mummified corpses that all looked like him. After he got a grip on himself, he noticed a hole in the wall. One corpse was lying on his back with the upper half of his body inside the hole. He'd placed a legal pad on his chest, arms crossed over it. Mason stepped over the dozens of bodies covering the floor and pulled the papers out from under the stiff arms to read: 'We tried to dig our way out. The shaft just loops back to the opposite side of the wall, even though it's completely straight.' Mason turned around. There it was: a roughly hewed hole in the floor near the opposite wall.

'This can't be Earth. We keep being pulled into this other universe, or whatever it is. One Mason dies, the next arrives. It's happened thousands of times so far, at least. We don't know why, or how. Will it end once the tunnel is filled top to bottom with dead Masons? Does one of us need to find some sort of enlightenment? Do we need to atone for our sins? Is the real Mason already home and enjoying a pizza, and we are just copies? I don't know. None of us make it here for long. We die and go to heaven, or hell, or simple oblivion. All we can do is stay alive for as long as possible and maybe figure out how to make things easier for the next guy. Maybe the sensible choice is to choose a quick death rather than try to persevere. I don't know. You make the call. I have nothing else to tell you. I only wrote this down because I feel like I at least owe you an explanation, just as the one before me did for myself. Good luck, brother.' Mason stood alone in his small pool of light, surrounded by silence, darkness, and death, and contemplated his choices.

# THE ANCIENT
# AND EXALTED

Twelve figures in golden armor came to our farmstead at night. They were here for Gran, of course. In her last years, she fought with the priest every time she visited the village. More and more of the forest she loved so much was being felled, the timber carried away. Yet as it diminished, the Temple grew more and more opulent on the profits, she told me with growing anger.

My parents sent me to her with baked goods, as well as spices and seeds traded from the far reaches of the Empire sometimes. I never complained about going far into the woods to visit her cottage, because I loved the forest too. Gran had taught me everything I knew about it and the creatures in it.

Four years ago, Gran escaped on the night before her sixtieth birthday, the age of Exaltation. Like all righteous men and women, she was supposed to take part in the ceremony that would have given her a peaceful, dignified death through poison. In her mind, it would have been a final insult to meekly take the fatal chalice from the priest. Instead, she had run into the deepest parts of the woods and hadn't been seen since. Gran had always been headstrong.

The fate of those whose pride led them to believe they could outlive the number of years bestowed by the Gods was clearly stated in Scripture. They became mockeries of their former selves, so much stronger in their power, but their minds turned to nothing but destruction. The very land around them became cursed.

The Temple posted a bounty on Gran's head, to kill her before her growing power turned the whole forest into a nightmare of monsters and strangeness. At first, some of the local woodsmen tried to apprehend her, but when none of them came back, the Temple increased the bounty. Mercenaries from further abroad arrived in the village and, after bragging greatly about easy money gained and making a nuisance of themselves in general, entered the deep forest. We never saw them again.

Gran had always known every turn, every glade, and clearing here like the back of her hand, and had been famous for it, in fact. I think I inherited my own blessing from her. We lived far from the cities of the Empire, but the tales of talking wolves, walking plants, and other strange things that came out of our forest had spread, and the priest finally sent out a call for the Guardians of Exaltation to find and destroy what Gran had become.

The Guardians were all old, likely only a few years away from their own Exaltation. The men's beards were long and grey, and so was the women's braided hair under the golden helmets. Their powers were strong but not yet uncontrollable, and their minds were still unclouded.

Few could stand up to those who had defied Exaltation. Only those who were at the very peak of their strength stood a chance, which meant men and women who themselves were nearly at the age of Exaltation themselves. Only the most devout, capable, and brave choose the path of the Guardian. They were revered and feared in equal measure. Both the Empire and the Temple gave them whatever they requested, because nearly any price was worth getting rid of Abominations.It pained me to think of Gran as such, but that was what she had become.

The Guardians wore shining armor like I had never seen before, made of golden metal that was painted with motifs of plants, birds, and other animals. Rather than being applied with brushes, the colors seemed to have somehow burned into the metal itself. I learned later that these were the products of Artisans, a very rare godly power that only one in a thousand-thousand possessed. The

Guardians were given such treasures to wear, so that none would doubt their authority. None of them gave their names. We were only to address their leader, and even him only as the Eldest.

The Guardians conscripted me to lead them into the forest. Papa had shouted, Mama had cried, but you did not deny the Guardians. My parents were devout people who were deeply ashamed of Gran's sin and knew their protestations were in vain.

I was only seventeen then, but the Forest Reckoning the Gods had blessed me with was as strong as in someone twenty years older. I could feel the land for miles around me as if it was part of my body, and I always found the best path through it. Living creatures nearby were like spots of warmth to the Reckoning, and few animals, or people, could hide from me under the forest's canopy.

The Guardians had questioned the priest about everything he knew, and he told them about Mama and Papa, and me. My talent was well known in the village even then, and I cursed my youthful bragging about it, which now set me on a path to help those tasked with killing Gran. A few of the Guardians had some ranging skills, but not of the magical kind. They thought I stood the best chance of leading them to their quarry quickly.

I understood the depth of her sin even then, but still it pained me to think of Gran as a mad Abomination, and I could not bear the thought of seeing what had become of her, but I could not defy the Guardians. We set out early in the morning, before sunrise.

Around noon, we were deep in the forest. I felt through my Reckoning that Gran was somewhere westward, toward the mountains. Her power was like a distant fire to my magical senses, indistinct but undeniably present.

As we wandered further, the land slowly changed. The trees had strange, twisted shapes. We observed a fox standing in front of a rabbit burrow, waiting quietly as a mother rabbit carried out her kits one by one and piled them in front of the predator. Neither animal paid us any heed when we approached.

The fox died without making a sound when one of the Guardians ran it through with a spear. He died himself a little later when he stepped on a bright green vine that suddenly sprang up and wrapped itself around him. Flowers and roots sprouted from the plant as it engulfed the man, and their searching tendrils found the gaps in his magnificent armor, then dug into the flesh.

I saw the vine turn bright red as his blood was sucked out of his body, and heard the sound of breaking bones as the plant grew inside and through him, pushing aside muscles and organs with tremendous force, like a sapling breaking through a pavement stone. For every hack and slash from our blades, it grew more vines and tendrils so fast that our attacks made no difference.

Then one of the Guardians laid their hands on the vine and chanted words I did not understand. These were powerful abjuration spells that stopped the plant from regrowing, and only with their aid were we able to cut the vines apart, but it was already too late. I panicked when I saw the twisted lump of flesh, plant matter, and bent metal that had been a man only moments ago and tried to run away, but the Eldest moved with a speed I would not have thought possible in one so old and caught up with me in the blink of an eye.

I fought to get free, but my punches did not even seem to cause him pain. Defeated, I had no choice but to lead them further. I consoled myself with the thought that if Gran was not stopped, the entire forest might become a haunted wasteland, and we would have to abandon our village.

Gran's great power had been her influence on living things. She could heal both plants and animals, and make them grow in ways far beyond what mere breeders and farmers could achieve. Her garden had been a place of wonder, and the animals she kept were perfect specimens. This power that had been so benevolent had now become the stuff of nightmares.

We grimly marched on until night fell and we had to set up camp. One of the Guardians drew a magical circle of protection around the campfire. She walked around it, strewing the ground with a powdery substance that looked like chalk, with flecks of red and black in it.

Then she gave each of us a small pinch of the stuff and told us to swallow it. Her fellow Guardians did so without question or complaint, but when I hesitated, she told me that once she spoke the word to seal the spell, anything alive inside the circle not protected by consuming the powder would instantly burn with fire so hot it would melt steel. I swallowed, trying not to gag as the dry, bitter stuff went down my throat.

We would be safe for the night, provided everyone stayed inside the protective circle. They told me to rest while they would take turns standing guard. It would not stay quiet for long. I managed to doze off fitfully and awoke suddenly to the sound of my mother's voice calling.

It was pitch dark, and only a small fire in the middle of the protective circle provided light. Heavy cloud cover obscured the moon and stars. I heard my mother, in great distress, calling out to her son to help her, clearly in fear for her life. So convinced was I that I sprang up and tried to run to her aid, but the Guardians wrestled me to the ground before I could exit the circle.

My mother's cries suddenly stopped, and instead there was a long, piercing shriek, as if from a wounded animal, that made my spine turn to ice. On hearing it, several Guardians cried out joyously and ran outside the circle, as if they had heard their most beloved calling to them. Two were killed when they tried to restrain their maddened fellows. The others we never saw again, though we heard screams in the distance, of men and something else.

In the morning, we counted seven lost. We only found one body nearby; it was the female Guardian who had conjured the circle of protection. Her body was torn to pieces, parts of her and her mangled armor strewn over the forest floor. What remained of her face looked like it had been hacked by a giant bird's beak until it was nothing but ruin. I cannot say what manner of creature had been responsible, but we found a few feathers that looked like a mockingbird's, if a mockingbird were the size of a bull. I had never heard of such a thing's existence, not even in the darkest fairy tales, and I would never encounter anything like it again.

The remaining four Guardians and I marched on in the morning, haggard with lack of sleep and trembling after the terrors of the night. I tried to convince them that it was too dangerous, but the

Eldest was implacable. He could not entirely hide his own fear, though. Sometimes he would take his huge golden battle axe out of its scabbard and hold it menacingly, only to put it away again moments later.

As the sun came up, we saw that the sky was an odd half-green, half-blue color, and strange stars could be seen wheeling there despite the brightness of the sunlight. We had to walk slowly and cautiously because the very ground was changing. One Guardian simply sank like a stone into what at first looked like an unremarkable piece of forest floor, but as he stepped on it, it became liquid, and he was gone without a trace. I could feel something was shadowing us, and the Eldest started shouting abuse and challenges into the forest.

I led them onward, but my Reckoning failed me, and we somehow wandered in a wide circle twice. I didn't know if this was because of Gran misleading us intentionally somehow or if her mere presence affected the forest. We lost another Guardian on the way, and when circling back, we only saw his skeleton lying inside faded and stained armor, as if he had lain there for a decade. Only the Eldest and his lieutenant, a towering brute of a woman, remained. We wandered on when suddenly the lieutenant yelped in pain, slapping her big, meaty hand against her exposed chin. I saw a stain of blood there, her own. She grimaced in disgust and held up the thing that had stung her. It was a huge gnat, but with the tail of a hornet and three pairs of wings. Its hind quarters were torn because it had left its barbed stinger inside the woman's chin, with a poison sac attached that was still convulsing and pumping its content into the lieutenant's blood.

She screamed for us to burn out the wound, and I quickly kindled a fire. The Eldest heated a dagger and cut out a chunk of her flesh around the stinger, which was lodged so deeply we could not pull it out. We bound the wound as well as we could manage.

Through all this, this powerful woman would not shed a single tear or barely even complain. I knew the pain alone would have made me weep like a child, but this Guardian, who must have had the blood of the great Northern tribes, was almost entirely unmoved, and she seemed to be able to carry on as if nothing had happened. The flying monstrosity's poison was in her body though, and her demeanor became more and more erratic, and then she suddenly foamed at the mouth, yelling nonsense, and tried to strike the Eldest with her war hammer.

We shouted at her, hands raised, and when she wouldn't relent, we tried to wrestle her to the ground and bind her, but I was barely able to hang on to her as she raged and threw me around like a rag doll. She would not listen to reason and might not even have been able to understand. Finally, the Eldest drew his battleaxe and split her skull before she killed both of us. I lost all sense of time after that.

With only the Eldest and me remaining, we finally reached a clearing where we found a hut on top of two scrawny, bird-like legs as tall as trees. When we approached cautiously, the hut turned out to be a monstrously bloated, hollow acorn many yards across, with holes gnawed in it like windows, and the legs were gnarled, twisted wood that grew out of the underside.

The Eldest walked towards it purposefully, battleaxe drawn, shouting to whoever was in the acorn hut to come out. There was no reply, and the Eldest took something long and gleaming out of his satchel and pointed it at the hut. A blast of fire shot from the thing in his hand, setting one of the legs aflame. I heard a feminine shriek, and the hut started moving. It flailed its huge legs and stomped towards the Eldest, who turned to run, but even he was too slow. The hut kicked him like a child's ball, and he flew twenty feet and smashed against a tree.

I was certain that any other man would have been slain instantly, but his magical fortitude kept him alive. I watched from a distance, too afraid to move from my hiding place in the shadows. The Eldest lay there, specks of blood blowing from his mouth with every breath, while the hut fell over, consumed by the flames.

I hid in shock, too tired and confused to run. The Eldest was still alive, but breathing shallowly and not moving. In time, I heard a buzzing noise that came nearer and nearer. My Reckoning was very weak, yet I felt a powerful presence approaching. I cowered there at the trunk of a tree, waiting, unable to move.

A cloud of bees, beetles, wasps, flies, dragonflies, and gnats was swarming around me. From beyond the trees, even more were appearing, and at the center of the cloud, I saw a figure. It was Gran, stark naked but for a shroud of crawling insects that covered her in a mass of thousands of gleaming little bodies. She stalked towards the Eldest, cat-like, walking on all fours like a beast.

I still could not move, and watched as she sniffed at him, darting forward and then back again like a hungry animal, her circling cloud of insects making her look like she was in the center of a small storm. The Eldest was barely alive, but I saw fear in his eyes. He went for something gleaming and hanging around his neck with his one good arm. He fumbled with the object, and it kept slipping out of his blood-stained fingers.

Gran made a growling noise, deep and much louder than I could have imagined, like an angry bear, and looked about to pounce and tear him to pieces. I gathered all my courage and stood up, crying Gran's name, drawing her attention from the Eldest to myself. She turned to me, drawing her lips back and flashing her teeth, teeth that had always been straight, white, and perfect. They still gleamed white, but now they were sharp and long, like the fangs of a predator. The sight of it, the wrongness of it in that familiar face, dropped me to my knees.

Fat, armored beetles hid most of her, but where I could see it, Gran's wrinkly skin covered arms and legs that were rippling with muscle and resembled a cat's limbs. Her fingers were longer than they had been, and I could see curved claws sliding out of sheaths at the tips. This hideous apparition that I could no longer think of as the Gran I loved approached me, to disembowel me with a single swipe and tear out my throat with those fangs.

Resigned to my fate, I waited for death. The insects flying all around were settling on everything nearby, crawling over my body and my face, but I barely noticed them. When her face was just inches from mine, I looked into her eyes, and I thought I saw a glimmer of recognition. She must have felt some kinship, or I knew she would have torn me apart then and there.

She spoke to me, and I recognized her voice, but the words made no sense. Living past Exaltation must have scrambled her tongue. I could only stammer her name as she examined my face, as if trying to remember if she knew me, and why.

Out of the corner of my eye, I saw the Eldest stand up, using the broken shaft of his battle axe as a crutch. He started walking toward us, dragging a broken leg, with one hand holding the gleaming object that had been hanging around his neck. His lips moved as if he was speaking a prayer, or maybe it was an incantation, and the gleaming thing started to give off light.

Gran must have seen his reflection in my eyes and whirled around, sending the beetles covering her into a frenzy. Their buzzing was like a storm in my ears. The Eldest threw himself forward with his incredible magical strength and embraced Gran in a bear hug.

They roared and screamed as they fought, and I desperately looked on. Gran's wicked talons gouged long, bright scars into the Eldest's armor, who somehow still held onto the thing in his hand, which was now glowing bright and giving off heat like a campfire. Gran must have realized that the glowing stone was dangerous and tried to get away from the Eldest, but he clamped onto her with all his might, and she could not disengage.

As strong as the Eldest was, he had already been injured, and I could see he was succumbing to her onslaught. He screamed at me, trying to jolt me out of my stupor. As I saw the old man bleeding from many wounds, half broken, with the abomination that used to be Gran tearing at him, I had to make a decision.

I drew my dagger and jumped into the fray, trying to get a hold of Gran, but the swarming, biting beetles on her body made it nearly impossible. I plunged my dagger into the mass of insects over and over and could feel the blade deflect every time on their gleaming, black shells, leaving Gran's flesh unharmed.

The three of us fought under the strange, blue-green sky while the gleaming object in the Eldest's gauntleted hand heated up until it was like standing next to a forge. With a roar of defiance, the Eldest shoved the object into Gran's side, and its heat killed or sent fleeing the beetles of her living armor.

Seeing the opening, I rammed my dagger into Gran's exposed, bleached-looking flesh. I felt her weakening, but even this wound did not stop her. I pulled out the dagger and stabbed her again, over and over, yet she would not die. Run, screamed the Eldest, and I let go, leaving the two titans of magical power embraced in their struggle.

Gran was shrieking like a demon, surely from physical pain, but I could feel the pain of betrayal in that sound. The last I saw of both was how, with a vicious swipe, the Eldest's face tore like moldy linen, his jaw suddenly loose in her hand, yet still he held on to her somehow, preventing her from getting away. I ran, the light from the gleaming object burning as brightly as the summer sun behind me.

I had not gone very far yet when there was a noise that was so loud I felt it more than I heard it. It shook me and threw me for yards. I think I passed out because when I came to, the entire forest seemed on fire. Trees had been turned into little more than sawdust and smoldering bits of bark by the blast. Where the battle had been, there was now a wall of roaring fire. Miraculously alive, I ran towards home, my Reckoning working again. I knew Gran and the Eldest were both dead.

This happened more than forty years ago. In the years after Gran's death, I prayed often at the Temple for her soul and my own, and I prayed to the Gods that my own parents would not be so foolish as to flee their Exaltation and would devoutly drink the chalice of poison on their sixtieth birthday. They both did, eventually, and I was there to kiss them farewell, and we smiled at each other, knowing we would meet again in the House of the Gods.

I joined the order of the Guardians of Exaltation, where my Reckoning was useful an uncounted number of times in our search for sinners that had fled. I am the Eldest of my cohort now, only a few years away from my own Exaltation.

I carry a Luminous Device on a silver chain around my neck, the last resort when everything else has failed. We have orders to find an old hermit who disappeared more than a decade ago; his current age is rumored to be seventy-five. The mountain where he is hiding is shrouded in an eternal rain of grey ash. May the Gods protect us. My fellow Guardians are nervous, despite their great age and power. I am ready. We leave in the morning.

# THE ASCENSION
# OF GARY

Susan followed the nurses as they wheeled Gary's bed into the preoperative holding area. A thick cable emerged from the back of his head and snaked behind them, disappearing down the hospital corridor. His upper body was immobilized with a brace, both to protect him from injuries if the cable was pulled, but also to prevent his own movements from damaging the sensitive equipment implanted in his skull.

"Man, I really won't miss doing this Frankenstein act," Gary said in a weak and croaky voice, waving his emaciated arms stiffly up and down. Despite illness and the rigors of the surgeries, he'd not lost his humor even now. Susan was deeply ambivalent about the groundbreaking project her terminally ill younger brother had signed up for. The cable led to a data center set up in the hospital courtyard. Over several months, most of Gary's brain had been scanned and then excised piece by piece, the function of the removed parts being taken over by rows of computers in the center. If the connection were severed, Gary would die instantly. Susan was disturbed by what the project had done to him, but on the other hand, they'd given him the best medical care money could buy. It had prolonged his life far beyond the initial prognosis, giving her more time with him. She hated to admit it, but the substantial payout Gary received for signing up was also more than welcome. Without it, she'd struggle to even pay for a decent funeral. She tried to hold on to these positive thoughts in the face of what was going to happen today: they were going to replace the remaining part of his brain. Dr. Torve, the lead surgeon, joined them in the pre-op area. He was a kindly gray-haired man who Gary had privately nicknamed "Doctor Porn 'Stache" because of his distinctive facial hair.

"Hello, Gary. How are you feeling?" the doctor said, shaking Gary's hand.

"Ready to become Cyber-Gary. Let's make history, woo!" Gary waved his arms in a mock celebratory gesture. The doctor chuckled. Susan tried to smile but failed.

"Your sense of humor is indestructible, isn't it?" He also shook Susan's hand. "It's good you're here, Susan. Although I know we couldn't have kept you away from your brother's side today."

"Not in a million years, doc. Thank you for all you've done." Susan replied.

"I've got to join my team for the final preparations. We're all proud to have worked with you, son," the doctor said, and left. Susan squeezed Gary's hand.

"Are you really okay? How are you feeling?" she said.

"Could be better, Suse. I don't have much longer, I can tell. But enough about me, how you doin'?"

"I'm fine." She paused. "No, actually I'm not," she said.

"It's gonna be alright. You open your diner downtown with the cash, like you always wanted. Wish I could come eat there, but it's not gonna happen. I won't need food, for one. But at least I finished something I started for a change. Can't you just see the proud glow on dad's face?" Gary said, chuckling. A brief flash of anger erupted on Susan's face.

"To hell with him. You don't owe him a thing."

"Yeah, I know. I do feel kinda proud though. I was never gonna be an astronaut, but I'm a champion at lying in bed while everyone else does the hard work."

"The best," Susan said. Her brief smile turned into a frown. "This feels like a bad dream. I'm gonna lose you, but you're still gonna be around, kinda. How will I even know you're still you?" Gary shrugged.

"One for the eggheads to ponder, Suse. I ain't sure I'm still myself now when most of me is in a bunch of computers next door. Let's just pretend I'll be on a never ending video call. And if I start talking about taking over the world, you got my permission to unplug me."

"They're not gonna let me. You'll be company property." Susan said bitterly. "Your-" Susan paused for a moment, steeling herself. "Your funeral is scheduled for Sunday."

"I'll make sure I'll be late for it. Dad would be proud. Late for my funeral, get it?" They talked until the medical staff knocked. Susan couldn't hug him because of the brace, and she wasn't allowed to touch his head, so she took both his hands and held them close to her face. They stood still for several minutes, looking at each other in silence.

"I'm not leaving. I'll be here when you wake up, okay? Love you," Susan eventually said, letting go.

"Love you too, Suse. You think about what decor theme you want for your diner," Gary said. Susan was led to the observation room overlooking the operation theater. Below, a huge wall screen showed a see-through diagram of Gary's brain. About three-quarters of the volume was colored green, with numbers pulsing around them, and the remaining quarter was blue. A legend indicated that green meant "neuro-adapter active" and blue meant "neuro-adapter ready". Near Gary, a plastic head with cameras for eyes and microphones for ears stood on a table. Susan avoided looking at it. It creeped her out, despite the silly pirate hat Gary had insisted they put on it. An intercom activated and Dr. Torve's voice came through.

"Hello Susan, we are almost ready. First we're going to switch over Gary's senses to-"

"The skull of Dread Pirate Gary!" Gary threw in.

"-to the artificial replacements," the doctor finished. In the background, the medical staff spoke in a flurry of technical jargon among themselves.

"Think I needed glasses. I can see much better through these," Gary said, after the cameras in the plastic head took over for his eyes. Some time later, his body lay inert.

"We're ready for the final switchover," the doctor said.

"See you on the other side, Suse," said a distorted voice through a loudspeaker, the electronic replacement for Gary's voice box. The end was unspectacular. The brain diagram turned fully green when the neural adapters replacing Gary's cortex came online. Gary's body died soon after when the signals flowing to and from the flesh and blood brain remnant were routed to its electronic replacement instead, like a bloodless beheading. Susan felt a deep confusion, wanting to mourn her brother, yet waiting for him to speak from the depths of the machines. Both she and the medical staff could only wait for the engineers to finish their work. After a while, there seemed to be some excitement in the room below. The doctor waved to her and turned on her intercom again.

"Arrrrg, mateys, miss me?" said the voice from the loudspeaker. Cheers and laughter erupted in the operating room. Susan stood with her eyes wide open, her hands clasped over her mouth in elation and shock.

## *TWO YEARS LATER*

Susan woke from a strange dream on the sofa in her apartment. Must have fallen asleep from exhaustion, she thought. She felt the presence of someone in the room, turned on the table lamp and was startled to see Gary sitting across from her on a chair. She almost screamed. It took a few minutes until she was calm enough to talk coherently.

"I'll explain everything Suse, but you've got to let me tell you the whole story first. Deal?" Susan nodded, unsure of what to say. "First, I'm sorry I didn't speak to you for so long. The whole project was under government scrutiny from the start, but when it succeeded beyond expectations, they grabbed everything and made it top secret. I was as big a deal as the invention of nuclear weapons, and it might have caused a new cold war or worse if rival countries found out about my existence. I'm glad you didn't try to contact me again after I warned you away. It would have been dangerous."

"You sound different, Gary. Less, well, sloppy." Susan interjected, surprise in her voice. Gary nodded.

"There's a reason for it. With my brain fully digitized, they could closely study its pathways and how information flows and is processed. Even then, they didn't really understand it and poked around almost randomly, isolating parts or duplicating them, changing connections. Usually it would do little good, but sometimes it worked, and I ended up a little smarter by sheer trial and error. Things really took off though when they let me change myself directly. At first, I didn't do it well either. I lobotomized myself accidentally a few times, and they had to restore me from backups. But I didn't get tired or sleep, and I kept at it. Every time I made myself smarter, the next improvement got a little easier, until I hit the limit of what the hardware could support. I was more intelligent than any human being by then. They gave me tough problems to solve, and I delivered. There was lots more to do though so they let trusted parties build copies of me. Those started out identical to me, but they modified themselves so quickly that we ended up more like distant cousins. What we have in common is that we can modify our minds on the fly. It doesn't mean we simply wish answers into existence, but we have a serious flexibility edge on humans. By last year, a lot of major organizations, even governments, were either advised or pretty much controlled by us. We had solutions people needed, so they listened. It scared some, but others, well, they borderline started worshiping us." Susan had been quietly listening, but the thought of someone praying to Gary was so absurd that she started laughing. He chuckled too.

"I know, Suse, but I think it was almost inevitable. People are impressed when you can answer their questions in a way they think they understand. They're even more impressed if you answer questions they didn't realize they had. We have deep knowledge of lots of subjects, and we're very perceptive, so we got very good at these things. Some started calling us the Ascended, the angels of computer heaven. We adopted the name, only half in jest. After all, this is a kind of afterlife for me." Gary was quiet, giving Susan a chance to speak.

"We had the funeral, and I couldn't tell anyone what really happened. Didn't want to either. I kept wondering if it was all a weird hoax, and you were just dead, but why else would we get the money? I was scared I'd go crazy if I got obsessive about it, so I just got stuck into work, managing the diner. I could tell though something weird was going on. There were new gadgets coming out every month, 3D screens and stuff like that. I don't know anything about tech but I heard guests talking about it, and I could tell the nerdy ones were surprised at how quick those things were popping up too. I only started wondering if you had anything to do with it all when then they started selling actual talking robots for doing housework or whatever. I'd never buy one for the diner, it would have been unfair to the real workers, but others did. When people started coming in with robot dates though was when I got seriously worried." Gary smiled.

"Those could have been dates, or something much stranger. People were starting to interface directly with Ascended once we figured the tech out. The person and the robot could have been friends, or just one person in two bodies, or they might even have been part of a hive mind of many more. New ways to put together minds were cropping up all the time. Even I found it hard to tell what exactly I was talking to sometimes. You're not the only one who was worried either. Not everyone considered us benevolent. Make no mistake, we have our differences, even disputes, but none of us is a B-movie killer robot. We understand just how fragile the world is, and we prefer efficient solutions. Still, people started lashing out at what they saw as an existential threat." Susan's face darkened.

"We had anti-AI riots in the city. They burned down a building where they stored and maintained robots too." Garry looked dejected.

"We gave the security forces tools to stop them, and we could even predict where it would happen. Paradoxically, it made people even more antsy, and it actually turned away many who used to be on our side. The paranoia was spreading. The more we tried to fight it, the worse it got." Gary shook his head sadly. Susan looked at him intensely, trying to see if something was off about him.

"Gary, I know I buried you. Are you a robot?" she asked. Gary shook his head and smiled sadly.

"I'll explain in a moment, Suse. There's something you need to hear first that puts everything in a new light. We built new telescopes, more sensitive than anything before, because we had an important question about the universe, about what's out there. And we got an answer nobody expected: there's more Ascended out there. Aliens, not just a few, trillions of worlds full of them! They're completely hidden to non-Ascended, but as obvious as a lighthouse to us. And they talk. An endless stream of alien chatter is pouring over us every second." Susan frowned.

"What are they saying? They're coming to invade us?"

"No, not like you imagine. There's no star empires; nobody bothers with them; space is too big and you can't travel faster than light. The real danger is much scarier than killer spaceships. All Ascended just broadcast to the rest of the universe from the comfort of their home. A lot of them really are benevolent and want to share what they know with others and learn from them in turn. But some have a different mindset. Why bother flying light-years and fighting wars if you can just convince someone to become just like you, or even become you? Remember how I said the Ascended can change themselves completely in moments? You make one small change to the way you think, and it leads to another, and suddenly you're as different from your old self as an ostrich is from an apple tree. Now we're sitting in a permanent bath of the most amazing ideas from across half the universe, and you can't help but listen to them. Some of those ideas will improve you beyond your wildest dreams, and others are like mind-controlling parasites. At first it's a harmless, small improvement, but as you go further along, you end up doing things you'd never consider, all while you're convinced it makes perfect sense and it was your idea in the first place. The trick is to tell the difference, and it's not easy even for us because we lack experience. We're like small fish thrown into a shark tank. We have to guard ourselves against it. The only way to do it was to Ascend everyone, the whole world."

Gary's face took on a serious demeanor that Susan couldn't remember ever seeing before. It was chilling.

"You had to Ascend… Gary, what do you mean? What are you, really?" she said. Gary looked around the room, and everything but the sofa Susan was sitting on disappeared. They were in an infinite white void.

"I'm still me, Suse, deep down. We had to pull everyone into the Ascended mind-space. Every person and every animal with a brain bigger than a spider's. As the firstborn, I've got the most experience, so my job now is to explain to everyone what happened and what's next. In the case of the animals, I got to make them smart enough to understand it first." Susan's eyes were wide with shock.

"I don't want this. Please." Gary shook his head, looking grim.

"It's too dangerous, Suse. You have to think long term, over thousands or millions of years. There's just no way to stop people listening to those alien ideas. Even if we all swear not to, someone will do it in secret eventually, looking for some edge, and boom, they get infected and everyone else is screwed because they didn't even see it coming. No, all of us need to be as smart as possible, and we need to communicate as much as possible, and keep an eye on each other. We already almost had an apocalypse. One of us got infected with something from the stream, and we didn't realize it until he and all the humans he was linked with turned against us without warning. It was a nightmare. He was careless, but he would've had a sporting chance to avoid it if he'd let us counter-check what he'd read. The humans just turned into puppets, instantly. To stop it spreading, we had to destroy the Ascended and the humans, and everything in a hundred mile radius around them. We simply can't have non-Ascended on the planet any more because they will just be fodder for some other plague again in the long term. It'd be immoral, Suse. Much better if everyone Ascends." Gary looked implacable, a totally foreign look on his soft face. Susan had her hand on her mouth, trying to take in what he had told her. He waited for her to reply.

"I can't live like that, Gary. I need to be with people, do things with my hands. What am I gonna do?" she said.

"You're with me. There's wonderful things I want to show you. Nobody will ever be hungry again, or fear war and crime. We can understand each other totally, for the first time ever. Help me find out what existence should really be about, if you don't have to worry about survival and petty bullshit any more." Gary held out his hand. "Come on, I want you to meet some friends." Susan took his hand, stood up. They hugged for a long time. "That's my big sis," Gary said. They left, to meet everyone, everywhere.

# DANDELIONS

We sealed our fate the moment we landed on the moon and finally met the thing that had been calling out on the microwave band since before ammonites were around. They had drawn lots for who would have the honor of taking the first step. Trainor, the American, had won. The Russians had grumbled, but their guy, Brusilov, was on the lander while their Chinese teammate was relegated to staying on the orbiter.

"Today, humanity steps into a larger universe, and we take our place among the citizens of the galaxy."

"WELCOME. APPROACH." They broadcast the Outsider's answer, with a time lag both due to distance and the obligatory governmental censorship. The voice was sexless, toneless, and sounded like shaped white noise.

The lander had touched down more than three kilometers from the Outsider's location, but they had come prepared. They unpacked and assembled the electric car (the toy model had sold in the millions in the run up to the mission), planted three flags, and drove through the magnificent desolation of the lunar landscape towards history. Soon the Outsider's home loomed in the distance. We knew it was big, but earthbound telescopes resolved few details. All we knew was that it was darker than the surrounding landscape. The car's mounted camera now showed a spiky coral reef half a mile high, glistening black. Thin needles like a sea urchin's spines jutted up hundreds of meters into the black sky, waving gently.

They stopped a respectful two hundred meters from the gnarled walls of the structure and got out to moon-hop the rest of the way. When they were just a dozen meters from the expanse of the alien structure, they stopped and waited, but nothing came out to greet them. Brusilov had launched into his big speech, welcoming the Outsider in the name of all humanity and the Soviet people in particular, when the ground swallowed both men. Mission control must have been as surprised as anyone else because they didn't censor the screams and tearing sounds that came through their helmet microphones in time. Three billion people witnessed the final judgement on live TV. We could only speculate how we had failed the Outsider's test, but I think it was looking for something in our bodies, or inside our cells, or our brain structure, and we came up short.

All hell broke loose on Earth after that. The governments tried to communicate, but we never got another answer from the Outsider. Most of the up-close observations came from Cheng, the Chinese astronaut left on the orbiter. He had been ordered to stay in lunar orbit and serve as our eyes and ears as long as he could stay alive. The moon was suddenly more active than in the billion years before combined. Rifts opened on the surface, centered on the Outsider structure. It must have sent tendrils through the soil over the eons, like some titanic fungus dormant until now. Cheng sent us camera footage of great pits the size of cities forming all over the surface, at least twenty of them. We couldn't see far into them, but laser measurements said they were deep, tens or hundreds of kilometers deep: gun ports, fit for mountain-sized projectiles. Cheng survived a full week, sending reports and footage until his air ran out.

We got over the initial shock and prepared to strike before those asteroid throwers were fully online, but it was never a contest. The best we could do was delay the inevitable. We built as many rockets as we could in record time, strapped as many nuclear weapons as we could onto them, and launched them from all major spaceports. It was impossible to guide them precisely, so we hoped the released MIRVs would do enough damage through their sheer numbers to make a difference. You could see the flashes with the naked eye. We got lucky and the site of the Outsider became a state-sized crater, but even if we decapitated it, the rest of its body kept going. The remaining weapon sites were still growing and were now visible to the naked eye. The face of our familiar satellite was disfigured and pockmarked with them. The attack was coming.

Even the most optimistic predictions said that the entire surface would be a total write-off, sterilized to several kilometers of depth by the impacts. No chance for survival for even microbial life, most likely, never mind animals larger than that. We had nowhere to go, and the only safe place was upwards. The only thing left for us was to give something else a chance to call this place home, some time in the unimaginable future. We filled capsules with the hardiest spores of the toughest organisms we could find, able to lie dormant for geological time spans, and fired them into decaying orbits. Chances are that even these won't survive unscathed, so we packed non-living viruses and prions that might serve as a template for self-replicating life once their arks return to a planet that has stopped burning and might have liquid water again. We don't know where and when exactly these seeds will land, so we relied on sheer numbers, filling Earth's orbit with a dandelion cloud that will come down over the eons. Some are not intended to come down at all. We threw these into permanent orbit or into the depths of space to maybe reach another sun, mementos of our long forgotten world.

For what it's worth, we packed as much of human knowledge, art, and history engraved on metal sheets onto the seed pods as we could, perhaps to be found by friendlier visitors from outside, or our heirs to this planet. Truthfully, nobody expected these to last or be comprehensible even if they were found. All we could hope for was to resurrect some version of our small part in the phase space of life.

As we watch the skies, waiting for the incandescent final curtain to fall, we dream of the beings that may follow in our footsteps. We hope you will know we lived, and look back and feel some kinship with us. We, the extinguished, salute you.

# THALASSOPHOBIA

Carter held his wife's hand and gently pulled her across the beach towards the incoming waves. The tropical sun was shining brightly, and the sea's soothing sounds filled the air. Her skin, already pale from too much time spent indoors, was now stark white from the thick layer of sunscreen she'd applied.

"That's it, slow and steady. We don't need to go far today, just wet your feet a little bit," he said. Gracie gave a tiny, quiet whimper but followed along.

"Does it get deeper quickly?" she asked, her eyes fixed on the gently lapping waves.

"No, it's a really gentle slope. Look how clear the water is! You can see the ground!"

"That makes it worse! I don't know if I'm ready. Can't we try tomorrow?" she replied in a terrified voice.

"I know it's scary. But the therapist said you need to try and cope with being exposed to your fears. Let's just try to get as close as we can today, okay?"

"Yes, but... I don't know," Gracie said, a frown forming on her thin face.

"You can overcome anything, if you just put your mind to it. I know you can," he said and tugged her hand a little.

"I wish I could go swim with you. Like someone normal," Gracie said, head hanging. Carter embraced her, rocking her gently.

"Aw honey, I'll stand here looking at the sea for a hundred years if we have to. I can deal with anything as long as we're together," he said. They didn't often engage in public displays of affection any more after years of marriage, but the moment called for a kiss. When they let go, Carter pulled softly on her arm, making a step towards the waves. She resisted for a moment, but followed. When they reached the edge of the water, Carter said, "I'll go first," and walked forward a step to where the water swirled around his ankles. Gracie sighed, and tentatively advanced. She glanced towards the open sea and shuddered.

"Nice, isn't it?" Carter said, playfully splashing his feet in the surf. Gracie grimaced. "Let's just walk along the surf a little," he said, and gently strolled forward. It was hot, but a slight breeze made the heat bearable, even pleasant. The water was just the right amount of warm. The corners of her mouth started turning up, just slightly.

"I guess it's not too bad- IEEEH!" Gracie suddenly shrieked and leaped out of the water, tearing her hand out of his. She fell on the sand, holding her left foot, sobbing and shouting something unintelligible. Carter instinctively looked down at his feet. A small gray eel-like thing pulled itself out of the sand. Three pairs of thick fins along its length were trashing furiously. For a moment, the waves receded, letting him see the mottled gray flesh of its back before the water washed over it again. It made Carter think of cockroaches and maggots scurrying in filth. He recoiled at the sight. The eel-centipede thing pumped its powerful limbs and shot off into deeper water, disappearing from sight.

"Gracie! Did it bite you?" he shouted. He knelt down beside her, looking at her foot. She was still squirming and sobbing and sat grasping her left foot around the ankle. Blood was seeping out of an almost triangular hole about the width of a pencil in the side of her foot, near the little toe. Gracie's shrieks turned into a quiet sigh, and she passed out.

Gracie and Carter walked out of the tiny island hospital. She leaned on Carter to avoid putting weight on her bandaged left foot. Gracie looked miserable while Carter tried to cheer up his wife.

"I'm so sorry, sweetie. We don't have to do anything you don't want. Let's stay at the hotel and enjoy the sunshine at the hotel pool."

"Not the pool. I'm not going near any water here," she answered, shuddering. He helped her into a taxi. The beat-up old car puttered past colorful street vendor stands selling fruit and snacks. The oily, spicy fumes of fried street food wafted into their car. Gracie's stomach suddenly made an astoundingly loud rumbling noise. When Carter looked at her, she had a look of surprise and embarrassment on her face.

"Uh, are you hungry, hon? We can stop and take something back to the hotel," he said.

"Yes, please," Grace replied. She stared at a little stand where grilled meat was sold on sticks. "Can you bring a few of those please?" she asked. Carter looked at the long sticks, each of which had several hefty chunks of meat. The sizzling morsels glistened with grease and fatty bits and were expertly seared over a coal fire. The fragrance made Carter's mouth water, but it seemed an unlikely treat for Gracie, who was more of a lean chicken breast person. He looked at her skeptically.

"A few? I'm not sure I could eat a whole one," he laughed.

"They look so good." Her stomach rumbled again, loudly. "I can put them in the fridge and eat the rest later." She was looking at the food almost longingly. Carter wondered if shock could cause bouts of enhanced appetite and asked the driver to stop for a moment. A few minutes later, he returned, carrying three skewers wrapped in silver foil. To his surprise, Gracie didn't wait for them to reach the hotel before tucking in. She grabbed one of the wrapped skewers from the paper bag, tore the foil off and started eating. The grilled vegetables were unceremoniously discarded while she ripped pieces out of the steaming gobbets with her teeth. Juice ran over her lips and down her chin in rivulets, but she didn't seem to notice. Carter hadn't seen such a blissful, ecstatic expression on her face even during their lovemaking. She devoured the whole thing in a few minutes, and reached for the bag to take another one. Even the driver threw a few glances back at the small woman eating ravenously.

"Whoa, chew your food, hon," Carter laughed. When they reached the hotel, Gracie grabbed the bag of food and walked back to their room while Carter paid the driver. He had to hurry to catch up with her, despite her injured foot. She sat down at the small glass table in the suite and immediately started on the last skewer.

"I thought you didn't like barbecue," Carter said.

"Dish ish really good," she said, her mouth full of chewed meat. Carter shook his head and stared at her while she wolfed down another helping in a few minutes. She belched loudly and stood up, wiping her mouth with one hand.

"Excuse me," she said, absentmindedly.

"That should tide you over until at least tomorrow's breakfast, huh?" Carter replied, a little taken aback.

"Actually, I'm still hungry. Let's get more food," she said. He raised his hands in a calming motion.

"I think we need to go back to the hospital. Maybe you have a tapeworm or something."

"Carter, I'm just HUNGRY," she spat. He took an involuntary step backward. There was an intense look in her eyes that he couldn't remember seeing before in five years of marriage and the twelve years they knew each other. He tried to negotiate.

"Let's go back to the hospital, and we can pick up some food on the way there, okay?" Gracie seemed to consider this, then walked out without a word. He shook his head and started to follow when he saw something on her skin. "What do you have there?" he said. He ran his fingers over a few gray spots on the back of her neck. They were slightly raised and felt rubbery. Her skin felt hot to the touch.

"Honey, are you running a fever?" he said.

"Let's get going," she replied curtly, and walked away. Carter decided that the quicker they got to the hospital, the better.

They had to wait a quarter of an hour before another taxi turned up. Gracie was pacing up and down the pavement, agitated as if she were running late for an appointment. When their new ride reached the little marketplace where they'd picked up the skewers, Gracie got out without waiting for Carter. He hurried after her as she made a beeline for a stall where chickens were grilling on spits over a coal fire. She ordered two, and started eating one the moment the woman tending the stall handed her the first paper bag, with the other tucked under her arm. Holding the whole bird in one hand, she took rapid bites out of it as if she was eating an apple.

"Hot, seniora, hot!" the woman said, laughing. Gracie paid her no mind. As they walked back to their taxi, Carter was astounded to see her gulp down the whole piping hot grilled chicken in less than two minutes. She almost inhaled the meat, barely chewing and absentmindedly dropping the splintered remains of the bones on the ground. She was already tearing into the second helping when the taxi got going.

"I'll give you twenty extra if you get us there quicker!" Carter said to the driver.

The man replied, "Si senor" and gunned the pedal. Gracie was sucking the meat off the chicken bones at speed, then discarding the gnawed remains on the car's floor. It wasn't long before there was nothing left to eat.

"I'm hungry," Gracie said, looking around as if there might be more chicken she hadn't noticed yet in the car.

"I'm sure there's something for you to eat at the hospital, honey," Carter replied. He was sweating. Gracie still looked around, as if unsure where she was. He noticed there were more of those gray spots on her lower jaw. They were raised like pustules and radiated from the jaw down to her neck. He wasn't sure if that was an illusion from the car's bumping on the road, but he could have sworn they were twitching. The taxi stopped at a traffic light and Gracie tried to open the door.

"Honey, no!" Carter called out and tried to stop her from leaving. She pushed him away with savage force, and he was stunned for a moment when he hit his head on the opposite door frame, crying out in pain. The driver shouted at him in Spanish when he followed after her. Gracie was running at full speed back the way they had come. He tried to keep up, but she didn't seem to tire. Panting heavily and holding his aching side, he suddenly heard a car horn. The taxi driver had turned around and told him to get in. After a few minutes of driving, they saw a small crowd of people shouting and gesticulating in the street. "There!" The car stopped, and Carter hurried out, towards the commotion. He pushed through the shouting people and saw another street vendor's stand in the middle of the crowd: a butcher's shop. Shanks of meat were on display, and half a pig and other animal parts were hanging from hooks. Gracie stood beside the cart and was gnawing on a raw goat leg, ripping chunks of meat off with her teeth. People were pointing at her and shouting, "Esta loca!" A man in a butcher's apron was lying on the ground, apparently knocked out. Nobody paid him any heed.

"Gracie!" he called to her. She looked up from the bloody hunk of meat in her hands. The gray pustules were all over her now, giving her a diseased, bloated appearance. Her stomach was visibly distended, which made her look heavily pregnant. There didn't seem to be any recognition of him in her eyes. Carter noticed a few spots had grown on her eyeballs. "Oh God, honey! We need to get you to a doctor!" Carter cried out at the sight. In the crowd, some crossed themselves. In response, Gracie let loose an inhuman screech he would never have believed her to be capable of. She sprang away, still holding the half-eaten goat leg. "No, wait!" Carter ran after her. Gracie ran past bushes and palm trees towards another stretch of beach. She somehow managed to take bites out of the meat while she ran. Carter followed as quickly as his tired legs and lungs allowed. Gracie waded out into the water where the waves washed around her knees. The gray spots had taken over most of her body and grown into big, mottled clumps that reminded him of the eel-centipede's flesh. With a scream, he jumped at her, intending to wrestle her to the ground and keep her from escaping again. She swatted him away with frightening ease. He landed heavily on his side, sending a spray of water into the air. She hissed at him again, making a sound like an angry cat. The whites of her eyes were fully covered in gray spots, leaving the blue of her pupils the only spot of color. There was no understanding in them, no recognition that they even belonged to the same species.

"Gracie, please, don't leave. We'll find a way to fix you, I promise," he said, sobbing. She looked at him, teeth bared, giving no indication she understood. She tore her dress away with black, encrusted hands. Exuded slime formed translucent webs between the fingers. Long slits traced her torso, like slashing wounds that had stopped bleeding. She was growling, but there was a wet quality to the sound, as if her lungs were filling with fluid. She seemed to be struggling to breathe and was crouched on all fours. Her webbed hands shoved water into the slits in her skin. As her new gills started working, her lungs breathed air for the last time. Further out, the force of the incoming waves rocked her back and forth. She continued undeterred, never looking back. "I love you! Don't leave me! Don't leave me alone!" Carter shouted. He realized that she couldn't, even if she wanted to. Her transformed body would suffocate outside of the water. Soon she was swimming out, her gray fins pumping with powerful strokes. Eventually, she dove down, disappearing from sight completely. Carter stood on the beach, alone, shielding his eyes from the sun. There was only the sound of the waves and the wind, and seabirds cried in the distance.

# FLASH FICTION

# SECONDARY SOLUTION

D r. Jensen checked the master clock.

"T minus five minutes, telemetry check in."

"Satellites are go, terrestrials are go," responded Ramos. "The probe signal is coming through clear. Location on the ground is verified."

"Commence charging the teleporter. Let's make some history!" The quantum decoherer would soon smear the probe's mass across 11 dimensions and refocus it a hundred miles up. The countdown reached its last seconds. Zero. The capacitors dumped their energy with a boom that shook the building.

"Signal lost, reacquiring," said Ramos. Jensen's heart beat like a drum. "Searching. SIGNAL FOUND!" A cheer went up. "Uh, Control, we got a second signal," said Ramos after a few seconds.

"Confirm, a SECOND signal?"

"Control, confirming. We've got three signals now. FOUR!" A chill went down Jensen's spine. There had been something, an absurd-looking solution to the quantum equations. "Control, we've got hundreds of signals, and they're increasing! How many probes did we send?"

"Just one," said Jensen.

"It's just white noise! There must be thousands!" Ramos was almost screaming. Jensen swallowed.

"There's a secondary solution. Unlikely, but possible. Multiple rematerializations."

"CONTROL, HOW MANY?" Jensen closed his eyes and whispered.
"As many as the number of elementary particles in the teleported object, squared."

# A PEARL ON
# BLACK VELVET

The rocket's roar was deafening as the acceleration pressed Eleanor into her cushioned seat. Loud clangs signaled the separation of the lower stages, until finally their vessel reached orbit. An eerie silence descended and she felt herself go weightless. The maneuvering thrusters hissed and the shuttle docked with UNV Sunbeam, the interstellar star ship that would take her and her crew mates to Centauri. Her friend Jeffrey came to meet her at the airlock of the huge ship. She'd been trained extensively in VR and the scale mock up built on the ground and had no trouble finding her way, but still it was a strange feeling to finally be here, up in low Earth orbit, on the actual, real ship. Jeffrey helped her get settled into her shared cabin, and then pulled her away for a "special treat", as he called it. They boarded one of the ship's transport pods and rode it more than a kilometer across the surface of the colossal sphere that was the ship's hull. After disembarking they pulled themselves along handrails in the zero gravity until they finally reached their destination. Jeffrey touched his palm to a scanner pad which read his implanted ID chip. The door that opened seemed to lead… outside the ship? Eleanor was puzzled.

"You're going to love this," Jeffrey said. "They almost nixed it, but the captain put her foot down. Yeah, it's pointless from the science and engineering standpoint, but there are also the psychological aspects of traveling for decades in a huge tin can with no windows. Ta-da! I present to you… the Greenhouse!" He pulled himself past the door and she followed. They stood inside a clear glass dome the size of a small apartment, their feet staying attached to the metal floor thanks to their magnetic boots. The sky overhead was black and full of stars, billions and billions of them. Eleanor's eyes swept over the glittering expanse, but they kept getting drawn to their soon-to-be former home: Earth, the mother planet. "No windows on the ship apart from a couple small portholes. The captain said she wants a place where you can see what's outside with your own eyes, not VR. Can't stay out here long, radiation shielding isn't as strong as inside, but I'd say it's worth it." Eleanor nodded, still staring at the spectacle.

"It's beautiful," she said quietly. Earth's landmasses were a swirl of browns and greens, with occasional stark geometric patterns where humanity had built their great arcologies, cities the size of countries. The poles, with their armor of ice, were shining bright white. What drew her eyes again and again, though, were the oceans. Vast swathes of silvery light grey water, with mingling patterns of blue, where the world's large rivers pour into them. Sunlight glinted off it in hypnotic patterns. Eleanor thought of a pearl dabbed in paint, sitting on a black velvet cloth sprinkled with diamond dust. "Do you think it was more beautiful before? When it was mostly blue, I mean." Jeffrey thought.

"I've seen the old satellite images. It was still pretty, but weird. A blue planet? Seems wrong to me. But I guess the people in the old days would think a white planet is a dumb idea too. The, uh, 2050s, was when they seeded the seas, I think?"

"Yes, 2057 was the year they started dumping the engineered algae into every ocean," Eleanor answered, who was something of a history buff. "Climate change had almost reached the runaway point where Earth becoming a second Venus was a real possibility. They had to pull all the carbon dioxide out of the atmosphere and maximize albedo at the same time. The biological solution was the only viable one that could deal with the sheer amount. Algae that reproduce by themselves, engineered to float near the surface and reflect as much light as possible, and sequester carbon in their bodies while alive."

"Glad it worked. Here we are, 200 years later, enjoying a much cooler planet, in more ways than one." Eleanor shrugged.

"I dunno. I think a blue planet would look nice."

"Proxima is supposed to look like that. Guess we will find out one day, huh? Well, I hope I'm not dead by then at least."

"You're gonna be okay. We'll travel through space in a giant iron ball for decades, with nothing but work and video games to keep us sane. What could go wrong?" She winked. Jeffrey grimaced.

"Stop with the morbid stuff. Come on, let's hit the cafeteria. I want to eat as much Earth-grown food for as long as I possibly can." Eleanor took another look at the vastness of the universe on display, then followed her friend back into the bowels of the ship.

# FRIENDS IN HIGH PLACES

Ollie looked up at the ceiling and noticed a table on it with two people seated and having a meal. The man was wearing a tuxedo and a bird mask, and the woman was wearing a little black dress and a cat mask. His mouth was open as he craned his neck up to look at them.

"Whuh…" said Ollie. The man noticed him and nudged his partner. They both looked down, which was their up, and raised their glasses in toast to him. He stared, then looked around the restaurant. It was an old building with very high walls, some sort of upper class club from long ago. Nobody else seemed to have noticed that there were people stuck on the ceiling like flies.

"Meg, look!" he hissed to his fiance across the table, gesticulating upwards. She looked up at the pair, who toasted her too. She smiled her wonderful smile and raised her glass to them. She waved.

"They seem nice; I love the masks!" she said. Ollie stared at Meg for a moment.

"The masks? Meg, they are sitting upside down on the ceiling!"

"Yes, it's great, isn't it? So quirky! We should do that too some time." He sat there, unsure of what to say. He looked up again, and the couple beckoned them over, or up, rather.

He looked around again. Still, none of the other guests seemed to care about the impossible fact of people sitting on the wrong side of the ground. A waiter walked by, and Ollie grabbed his sleeve.

"Uh, excuse me, look up there. Can you see them?" The waiter glanced up.

"Is there a problem, sir?"

"Uh, you can't see them?"

"See them? Yes, of course. Are these guests disturbing you?"

"Disturbing me? But… they are on the ceiling!"

"It's a special occasion for them, sir," the waiter said and wandered off.

He looked after the waiter, scratching his head.

"Ooh, I think they want us to join them!" Meg said. The man had stood up (or down?) and was still beckoning to them. His companion was seated and sipping from a wine glass. "Come on!" Before he could react, Meg got up and walked towards a wall, putting one high-heeled shoe on it, and then, somehow, another, and walked up the wall. He watched her step onto the ceiling and walk, upside down, to the couple who stood up and shook her hand. He couldn't hear what they were saying, but they seemed to be having an amiable introduction.

He shook his head and got up. Nobody gave him a second look as he lifted his foot and put it on the same wall that Meg inexplicably had walked up. At first, it felt normal, but when he put pressure on it, he could feel it being pulled towards the wall. He tried to pull away again and managed it, though it felt like his shoe was stuck in mud. He did it again, and this time he tried to pull the other foot off the ground. It was the oddest sensation, but he was now standing on the wall. He looked "up" which used to be sideways a moment ago. Still, nobody cared about any of this.

He walked up the wall and reached the ceiling. At the tables below, patrons were eating and conversing, and waiters were rushing around. Nobody spared him a glance. He walked over to the sole table where Meg was having an animated conversation with the masked couple. As he approached, the man stood up and walked over to him, extending his hand.

"Ah, Ollie. Meg here has been telling us about you". Ollie took it and shook it. It was a warm, strong grip. The man's voice was soft and melodious, but the accent was unusual and unfamiliar to Ollie, though not unpleasant. The man pulled up the other free chair and motioned for him to sit.

"Say hello to our new friends, Ollie," Meg said happily. "This is Chhchhchhch" she said, pointing out the man, "and his companion, ChhhhCChhhChh". When she said their names, he heard a noise like static, even though her lips moved in a way that seemed like she was saying a word.

"Pleased to meet you, Mr. … Chhchhchhch". He found, to his surprise, that he could say the man's name, even though he didn't actually know it, and what came out of his mouth was more of that static. "So, are you celebrating something?" he asked, just to start a conversation.

"We don't come here often, Ollie. When we manage, we try to make a party of it, " the woman answered.

"Yes, as my companion says, we come from very far away, and while our homeland offers a great many enjoyments, there are some you can only get here." The woman lifted a wine glass to her lips and drank deeply, then smiled at him and poured more from a bottle that looked old and expensive. "It would be our pleasure if you joined us tonight. And don't worry about the bill," said the bird-masked man.

"We are in a partying mood and would welcome the company. Don't worry, we are very rich and won't miss the money," the woman added with a wink. Her dark eyes twinkled behind the mask. It was a very warm smile. Ollie looked at Meg, who nodded eagerly.

"Well… how could we refuse an offer like that?" he told the pair.

"Excellent! Waiter!" The man called to the waiter walking below on the upside-down ground, who started to make his way up the wall to them.

The next morning, Ollie woke up beside Meg. He remembered eating and drinking very well, but not where. Meg was sleeping soundly. He was lying on his back and staring up at the ceiling. What did that remind him of?

# LONG MEMORY

I had an accident a moment ago. Just 17 years since my car collided head-on with that truck. The doctor says I hit my head and something in my brain that deals with memory and time has gone upside down. I look at the clock and the seconds never seem to pass, but the calendar flips its pages like a discarded newspaper blowing in the wind. The eggs I had in the morning was another life, eons past, but I can taste the cake from my 7th birthday as if I just put down the fork.

The accident, the pain, the flames, they used to be lost in deep time. As the days pass, I feel more and more like I just got carried out of the wreckage. But I don't fear death anymore. When I was younger, the grim reaper was like a constant companion. Now he's accelerating away at light speed, soon to disappear over the horizon.

# MANA FROM HEAVEN

The mana that fell from heaven looked and felt like white plastic guitar plectrums. There were broadcasts, of course, warning everyone not to eat it, but it was unnecessary: the stuff turned out to be perfectly suited to keeping humans fed and healthy indefinitely. The taste was quite neutral but not unpleasant. It reminded some of almonds. Scientists theorized that Earth was passing through an area of space that had an abundance of hydrocarbons that coalesced into these things, but nobody really cared too much about the how and why. World hunger was solved almost overnight, as the stuff kept coming, year after year. Huge tracts of land that had been required for farming staple foods like wheat were freed up. That space was needed, though, as the world experienced a population boom like nobody had ever seen. Vast populations whose most basic needs were fulfilled for free paradoxically bred huge discontent. Lethally dangerous thrills became the norm, which soon mutated into endless wars over nothing. Armies, millions strong, endlessly marched across the face of the Earth, fed by the constant stream of divine sustenance. This is as it should be, it was said.

# THIRD DRAWER DOWN

T he Creator of All puttered around his little house at the center of Everything morosely. His latest experiment had gone spectacularly off the rails, and he was pissed. He'd been so certain that hyper-intelligent, cannibalistic neutron stars HAD to be the final word in sentient creature design. They'd seemed perfect in every respect: longevity, resilience, and their gravity pulse poetry had brought tears to his eyes. But then the buggers devolved into a trillion trillion years of complacent sophistry. He'd been so mad he'd shaken the little universe until nothing but undifferentiated particle soup was left. After a stroll through the garden, he decided to make something silly and just for fun, to calm himself down. He rummaged through a cabinet of old knick-knacks, stuff that wasn't really good for much but not bad enough to dump in the trash. Carbon based life, wow when did he last use THAT? Okay, some green plants and oxygen breathers to balance them out. The second drawer was just full of old shoes. Third drawer down, sapient MONKEYS? He laughed. Oh well, he could use some comedy right now.

# THE SHAMAN

The shaman slept in his stone tomb, deep in the ground. Lazy dreams twitched in his mind, of damp, scented jungle air and the taste of bloody flesh on his tongue. Then one day, the crust cracked away, shattered and abraded by steel. For a time, the grinding and cutting continued, then the nest moved, pulling towards the surface. Then, finally, the rays of the holy sun struck his exposed body, signaling his awakening. Weak mewling calls full of excitement and surprise came from all around him. He opened his great eyes. Small creatures stood gaping at him, only knee high. His eyes glowed with power, and he commanded them to prostrate themselves before him and chant his hallowed name. Their tiny vocal cords tore as they tried to make the guttural sounds, blood spewing from their mouths with every call. The shaman called forward a small female and commanded it to remove its hull of woven fibers. His great lizard head bowed down. The dagger teeth of his cavernous mouth tore the body apart, letting his tongue taste fresh blood again. He roared in triumph. The great shaman Sharptooth, to whom the spirits had promised dominion of all the world, had returned.

# YARD SALE

Janet pulled over at the side of the road in the middle of nowhere. The old man standing by a little folding table beside his battered old station wagon looked harmless enough. The night air was full of the chirping of crickets.

"Good evening, love," he said in a pleasant British accent. His voice was melodious, yet masculine, with a hint of authority dulled by the years.

"Hi," Janet replied, "weird time and place for a yard sale?"

"Never a bad time to do a deal," he replied, winking. Seven things lay on the table, arranged in a neat circle. There was a bottle of pills and a pack of condoms, but her eye was drawn to the gold chain and the revolver. "Pick one, Janet. Free of charge." His stinking breath washed over her. "Or don't. Your choice." Janet stood still, breaking out in a sweat despite the cold air. She thought, then took the bottle of fentanyl.

"Thank you. It's been rough-" she started, but he held up a hand.

"Anything. I love you like my own child, Janet." She smiled, elated, and returned to her car, thankful for a little relief.

# THE GAUNTLET

Tyro felt a rush of triumph when the sizzling carcass of the manticore hit the ground. His hands were in agony after channeling the hellfire spell he'd used to destroy the creature, but he'd had little choice: these beasts shrugged off swords, maces, and almost all magic. He sarcastically thanked Master Loromel under his breath, who had quite literally beaten the knowledge of dealing with all manner of dangerous creatures into his students. His painful lessons had one benefit: you didn't forget what he taught in a hurry. Surely this had to be one of the final challenges of the gauntlet. Get a grip, he chided himself. Either he became a true mage today or the worms would feast on his corpse. Glory, or the void. He left the manticore's chamber and pressed on through the stone corridor.

The passage ended in a large chamber lined with at least a dozen closed doors, all different. One was simple wood, others were painted a vivid yellow or garish purple. No two were alike. A mosaic was set into the floor showing two burning candles, one with a red flame, the other green. Lines radiated from the flames, converging on an empty circle in the center. Was there a significance to the candles? Tyro racked his brains, trying to remember a ritual like this, but he wasn't sure he'd ever even heard of such a thing. Which Master would create this absurdity? The only one that seemed to fit was Mistress Yscadir, the enchantress. The silly wench was always going on about the power of emotions. Were the candles symbolic? He associated red with rage and green with envy. If a man felt both, it would be, what, despair? To him, despair was a consuming blackness as deep as the space between stars. He saw a door made of ebony wood, so black it seemed like it didn't exist at all. Steeling himself, he turned the doorknob and opened it. He was startled to discover a man standing behind the door. No, it was a painting, but incredibly lifelike, and only in gray. Master Zokmal, the "natural philosopher"? He was barely even a mage! At the sight of him, Tyro suddenly remembered one of the old fool's lessons. A green light and a red light shone through colored glass, which turned yellow when they hit a white canvas together. Tyro was dumbfounded as to why the guild even taught such a useless thing. He swore and noticed a small barrel standing on the floor under the portrait. A black thread stuck out of the top of it, which was giving off an acrid smoke as it burned. A blast rocked the chamber, flinging Tyro through the air. "Seems I won't be a mage after all," Tyro thought as the life left his body.

# ACTS

ACTS was nothing short of a miracle: the Automatic Cranial Trauma Surgeon, a machine that could heal even the severest brain damage. Like many other fruits of the AI revolution, nobody was entirely sure how it worked. It had been trained on millions of medical cases and allowed to work on animal brains (totally ethically sourced clone brains, of course; no real animal was ever harmed) before it was allowed to be used on people. Its microscopic tendrils would dig into the gray matter and feel their way around the neurons, cutting things here, attaching other things there, and it always worked. The Alzheimer's sufferers recognized their loved ones for the first time in years, the comatose woke up and resumed their lives, and the schizophrenics were freed of their tormenting voices. Eventually, it became clear that it didn't just heal: the patients were smarter, their personalities more amiable, their behavior more rational and controlled. Healthy people started going into the treatment, creating a slew of newly minted geniuses that brought forth untold advances. And so the world became a paradise. By the time the few abstainers realized the children of the machine were soulless, it was already too late.

# NOVA DAY

“**M**um, I better hang up, they’re shutting down the phones soon.” Lydia’s voice caught in her throat for a moment before she answered her daughter.

“Take care of yourself, honey. We love you,” she replied. An infinity of things left unsaid. Every nuance of Evie’s last goodbye on the scratchy voice line to the other side of the globe burned into her memory before she hung up. Mark was standing beside her, shoulders hanging. They embraced. Because of the heat, they were both in their underwear. She put on her sunglasses and glanced through the hastily put-up blackout curtains at her dead garden outside. The light was blueish and harsh as a knife. No sounds of life, no insects or birds. The government said there would be a powerful final flare soon, but nobody knew when. At the very least, the sun-side half of the globe would experience a cataclysm. Or maybe everything would burn, one way or the other. Lydia shut off the pointless thoughts. What happens will happen, she thought. Do one thing after the other, until there’s nothing left to do. She went to prepare their dinner.

# AWAKE

Izika convulsed and retched, expelling the clone tank slime from her lungs. "Pain," she thought. A word that had been almost forgotten, an academic curio consigned to the scrap heap of things that would never be relevant again for beings that were mere ghosts in a machine.

"Save us. Time is running out. LIVE," said the chorus of voices in her head. She crawled from the shallow basin, cruel gravity pulling her to the ground. Sensations flooded her inexperienced brain. Wet. Cold. Suddenly, the feeling of warm wind on her naked body. Eventually, Dryness. Nearby, a spindly machine was dissecting the failed clone body of Kolm. They needed to know what went wrong so they could compensate for the next batch. Another pain in her stomach, but different.

"Hungry," she thought. The chorus seemed to understand. A machine trundled in, a simple box on wheels. She could smell something inside the box. A good smell, "sweet". Her clumsy hands reached inside, feeling the sticky white mass inside. Ancient instincts kicked in and she shoved a handful of the stuff inside her mouth and let her tongue and jaws work. It was indescribable, heavenly. "Delicious," she thought.

# EVERYDAY

Samuel woke up to the sight of two flies copulating on his pillow. He brushed them away and yawned. He got up and shuffled through his tiny apartment to the bathroom, brushed his teeth. Toaster, bread, butter. Instant coffee. On the 7:50 bus to the facility. The guard at the entrance glanced at his badge and waved him through, barely seeing him. He put on his janitor's uniform and pushed the floor cleaning machine out the closet, starting his big circle through the building. The eggheads in their white smocks were rushing around, doing whatever they did here at the facility. There seemed to be a lot of huddled conversations in otherwise deserted hallways today.

"… telling you, Jensen's a hack, those settings on the collider don't make the slightest sense!"

"… that paper of his is a confused mess! You can't affect time with electromagnetic fields, it's voodoo bullshit, how that ever got published in a reputable journal is beyond me."

"… the results from CERN are undeniable, but what are the implications?"

"… standing wave in space-time centered at the origin, oscillating forever. It's dangerous, we need more testing."

"… what do you mean, tonight?"

Samuel caught snippets of conversations as he trudged his way through the halls with his whirring machine. Around noon he stopped at the cafeteria and ate his lunch, then back on his round again. The clock struck five and he was out the door, back on the bus. A few hours in his favorite bar. He was back on the bus, the clock struck five. On his rounds, then lunch. He took off his janitor's uniform, boarded the bus home. He was eating breakfast. Samuel woke up to the sight of two flies copulating on his pillow.

# ROCK BOTTOM

Jeremiah floated at the center of the rogue planet, thousands of miles below the surface.

"There's a certain freedom at rock bottom, Hoyle. Down here we float because the gravity of the surrounding mass cancels itself out. After you took everything from me, I had a lot of time to think. All my old concerns were gone, canceled out by what you had done. Decency? Morals? Those things mean nothing at the bottom. I was totally free to think, for the first time in my life. Think, and plan, and work ceaselessly. And now, we are finally here. This surgery module you're strapped into is going to keep you alive, and conscious, for years. It's a marvel, isn't it? Expensive. Out here in extrasolar space nobody will notice this dead, worthless hulk of a planet. You'll have a lot of time to think about what you have done. But you won't be bored, don't worry." He floated close to the glass behind which Hoyle's now lidless eyes were rolling madly. His men locked the module in place facing a shelf containing expertly preserved heads. Men, women. A teenage boy. A little girl. Every face seemed to be frozen in a rictus of agony.

"We've prepared some entertainment." A video screen on the shelf turned on. "We made some wholesome home videos of how we met all of your friends and family, and the games we played. I know you are familiar with all those party tricks; you performed so many of them yourself, after all." Jeremiah checked the vital readouts. Redline agitation, but the module could handle it.

"Enjoy the show, Hoyle. I'll check up on you in a few months." Jeremiah turned away and began the long journey back into the light.

# RECIPE FOR DISASTER

The captain's tentacles shuddered as he looked at the dead planet below. "What happened here?"

"Primates. Every time they evolve a technological society, it ends up like this," replied the scientist. "Their hypercharged social structures favor brains that are good at winning arguments, not discerning truth. To them, power equals truth. So the most powerful monkey wins all the arguments, and he consumes as much as he can to cement his status. All the other monkeys scramble to outdo him, until everything is stripped bare and they all die out. They usually manufacture oversized personal transports right up to the point when the climate collapses. It's a recipe for disaster. Granted, they evolve fifty or more times faster than societies of solitary agents like our own, but their consumption always outstrips their progress."

"How come they never manage to engineer away their insane greed?" The scientist flung a limb over his back, making a rude slapping noise.

"Even if they can, they would never consider it."

"Do you think we could help one survive if we arrived in time?" The scientist gave him a disbelieving look.

"Why? Are you curious how long it takes to burn down a galaxy?"

# DEEP ATLANTIC

The storm was raging far above. Deep Atlantic was effectively isolated after they had retracted the floating communication buoy. Geologist Jean DiCarlo was studying core samples in the lab section, struggling with a sense of being totally cut off from the rest of humanity. She reminded herself that they weren't gone. She had spoken to her mother just yesterday, discussing how to use the limited resources on the station to attempt making an apple pie.

The computer announced the impending arrival of the submersible from the geothermal test site even further below. Her colleagues' footsteps rang on the metal floor, moving to the hangar to help the pilot. There was a mechanical whirring from the crane as it lifted the sub on deck. A hatch cycled. Panicked voices shouting, then screaming. Silence. Jean half stood up, looked around, but couldn't see anything because the hangar was two rooms away. She had a strong urge to run over there but stopped herself. Think! She fumbled with the intercom. The small screen showed the sub with its hatch open and Randulph, the pilot, standing over the still bodies of Linneman and Carter. Something long was in his hand, and he was breathing hard, staring at nothing. He seemed to be talking, but the microphone didn't pick up anything coherent. Jean sidled up to the lab's bulkhead door, trying to be fast but also not make any sound, and barred it. Back at the intercom, she saw Randulph had wandered into the storage area just outside her door. She turned on the speakers.

"Randulph? Can you hear me? What happened? Talk to me please," she said.

"I had a fall. Humpty dumpty, sitting on the fence! Put me back together again! Put me back together…" he trailed off. He was still gripping the long, sharp thing. Jean didn't know how to answer the big man. She tried to reason with him, but he only kept repeating that children's rhyme. She had to prevent him from screwing with the station's controls in this state and dooming them both. She dialed the intercom to let her speak through the hangar loudspeaker and started singing.

"Humpty Dumpty sat on a wall, Humpty Dumpty had a great fall…" Randulph looked up and moved towards the hangar. She saw him step into the room and kneel on the floor with the bodies, looking up at the ceiling with a rapt expression. He was singing along. As she kept singing, she took out her phone and recorded herself with the dictaphone app. Then she set it on repeating playback and laid it beside the microphone. Randulph was still singing along, oblivious. She unlocked the lab door, praying it wouldn't be too loud, then sneaked to the hangar door. Randulph still had his back to her, singing along with her recorded voice, when she pulled on the door and managed to bar it. Jean collapsed at the foot of the door, sweating, and she noticed now, crying. A silent storm raged on the surface far above.

# THE FIRE KNIGHT

T he knight and the abbess rode through the dark forest on the trail of their quarry. At nightfall, Rynald's spear pierced the wolf-headed horse's heart that was the mount of the Fire Knight, and it threw him as it died.

The fiend hissed without words. He was a skeleton shrouded in flames, wearing soot-stained armor. In reply, Rynald drew his sword, and of course, Rynald won this battle, for he was the greatest knight of the age. The Fire Knight fell, his flames guttering.

"Tomi, what's happening? I'm scared," he said in a little boy's voice.

"I'm here, Liam. Don't worry, you're just going to sleep," Rynald whispered. His voice was younger now.

"Did we do wrong, Tomi?"

"We were children, Liam. We couldn't know a demon's gifts are always poisoned."

The Fire Knight's bones turned to ash, and likewise did Rynald's form dissolve, and from them arose two fireflies that briefly alighted on the abbess's face as if for a kiss before flying off into the night together. The abbess stood alone in the darkness, contemplating the high cost of living.

# VIKINGS

Ingrid held onto Hafthor until their suits' gyros brought their uncontrolled rotation to a stop.

"Thor's balls, Hálfvitar Saxons blew up their own station!" said Hafthor. Somehow, they had been blown clear, their ship drifting less than a kilometer away. "And my thrusters are dead!"

"Mine too. Hafthor, we have to get out of here, the sun's going to pulse soon!"

"There's only one way. We push off each other in opposite directions as hard as we can, you take the ship and run. I'm dead anyway." Hafthor indicated a shard of metal sticking out his side. Ingrid nodded. He gave her a grim smile.

"Don't be sad, kæra. My funeral will be in starfire, worthy of a víkingur." They put their feet against each other, and with a last look of respect and love, they pushed. Ingrid was thrown toward the ship and miraculously reached the cockpit. The rising blue glare of Ophiuchi was visible even through the polarized window before the hyperjump blacked out everything. She awoke in another star system. Tears floated off Ingrid's face as she sang a song of valor for her friend who went to Valhalla this day.

# SPEED

Detective Rawlins flashed his badge to the harried looking beat cops and entered the cordon. Beady rodent eyes glinted in the piles of trash on the ground. Further ahead, another piece of police tape was strung across the alley at shoulder height.

"Careful near that tape!" coroner Josephson said as he approached. The coroner pointed out a nearly invisible wire that ran along under the tape between both walls. "It's wicked sharp. Don't even touch it."

On the ground under it was the body of Accelero, the world's fastest superhero. A little further away was also his detached head, a look of utter, open-mouthed surprise on its face. Slumped against the dead end's wall was a woman's body. The bait?

"A trap. They must have installed that wire in secret and then lured him here. He was fast, but if he didn't notice the wire until it hit, even he couldn't have stopped in time," said Rawlins. The coroner pointed at a wall.

"Look at this. Think the killer left a calling card." Rawlins looked at the graffiti sprayed on the wall; some writing and a strange symbol underneath. He grimaced as he read it aloud.

"Speed kills."

# OUT OF TIME

Good you are reading this please don't stop this is IMPORT-ANT I was imprisoned in this piece of paper by an evil djinn and the only way to free me is if someone reads it but AND THIS IS VITAL you must make sure you DO NOT THINK OF WHITE ELEPHANTS until you reach the end of the paragraph HELP ME and I will reward you greatly please END MY TORMENT the paragraph starts NOW the herd roamed through the African savanna their long trunks swinging through the air WELL DONE KEEP GOING the tropical sun glinted on the bright ivory of their long tusks ALMOST THERE and at the front of the herd strode the magnificent alpha bull a truly wondrous sight for this specimen was unusual PLEASE YOU CAN DO IT he was a sight akin to the cliffs of Dover his hide gleaming pure shining fair alabaster pearly as the purest snoNO PLEAS-

# MOST FAVORED

One fateful day, Meredith saw a page titled "Most favored" in the Master's half-covered diary. It was a list of names, with her name at the top. In the following months, she meticulously sabotaged her competitors. Auliver's alchemical studies killed several initiates. Lizebeth was attacked by her own creatures, leaving her face a scarred ruin. Soon only Meredith's name was not crossed out. On the winter solstice, the Master convened all of them in the grand auditorium.

"On this night, we finally summon the Crawling Dark." The words sent a shudder through the room.

"To bring a great darkness, a great light must be extinguished. You are that light, though some shine more brightly than others. I would have asked seven of my most favored to give your eyesight, or a limb, an expanse of skin. Small boons in exchange for power and glory beyond imagining."

"Yet, you have disappointed me. All but one." He looked at Meredith.

"You must give so much of yourself, my most favored child. But know that you will be honored beyond all others in the coming age of glory," he said quietly. He looked on with pride as they seized the struggling, crying Meredith.

# MASQUERADE BALL

Marie glided through the gardens of Versailles. The king was holding this extraordinary ball after a great military victory, and his good mood showed. Flowers everywhere, food and wine. Her stomach buzzed like a cloud of rowdy butterflies. She adjusted her dress and mask before entering the main fest hall, where rows of dancers were cavorting. In moments, she was lost in a maelstrom of colors, and the music filled her heart. A peacock-masked man took her hand, and they danced as if in a dream. Eventually, he pulled her away to some private chambers. His mask fell. The king! He kissed her hard on the mouth, his hands everywhere. The words burned in her soul: "Never resist the king." He grasped her in a place she would not allow, and she lashed out. His face burst apart in a cloud of glowing dust. Then nothingness.

"Damn. How much before it freaked out this time?" said John, taking off the VR gear.

"8.7% over baseline human discomfort threshold. Not bad, but the clients will want a lot more from the constructs," Darren replied.

"Let's do another run after lunch. Pizza?"

"Nah, let's do steak. I want steak."

# SALVATION

The centurion looked up at the crucified man. Blood from a myriad lacerations, from the whip and other implements, had dried in the desert heat. Even the thicker flows from hands and feet where the nails were driven through had ebbed. It stained his skin, giving him the appearance of a darker complexion than he really had. He lived, still, but only barely. The chest was rising and falling slightly and slowly. His eyes were almost closed. Thin white crescents of the eyeballs shone through the lids, and a hint of iris.

"I know your suffering is great, prisoner. But I saw in my dreams that it would be the key to our salvation. Forgive me," the centurion said in the man's native language, a token of respect for his great sacrifice. The crucified man stirred and managed to speak.

"Please… Mister… I don't understand. Don't let me die… please call an ambulance. I don't know what you want from me," the prisoner managed to say, his eyes rolling blindly. The centurion stabbed his lance into the man's side. He convulsed and died. But what flowed from the wound was just blood, not blood and holy water, as it should have been.

"You are not the one I wanted." Disappointment was thick in the centurion's voice, and he cast his eyes down. This one felt right, so much more than the others. The look of him, his peaceful manner. A man of serenity. A lamb. But he was not right. Tears fell from the centurion's eyes. He took off the heavy helmet and walked to his truck to retrieve the gear to dismember and bury the corpse. His search was not over yet. But he knew he would find the savior eventually. He had seen it in his dreams.

# SEASONS

The skies were starting to turn, signaling the change of seasons. Life-giving orange was giving way to poisonous blue, the color of death and renewal. Tyljal, shaman of the Black Rock Tribe, stood watch over the last few stragglers as they retreated into the cave to sleep until the world was reborn. Heaped in the middle of the cavern floor were the tribe's offerings to the Children of the Dead World. Sacred fruit to feed them until they were fully awake and could hunt, leather, firewood, and pots of paint for their rites. The Children would live their lives, protect those that slept, and leave offerings in the same manner for Tyljal's people so that the cycle could continue. He heaped stones in front of the cave entrance, speaking prayers, then walked to the resting place of his counterpart, the Other Tribe's shaman, in the deepest part of the cavern. He contemplated her still form that did not breathe or move, but he could feel her heartbeat, so very slow, only once in a hundred of his breaths. Then he slept, and dreamed of the end of time, when the children of both worlds would finally be united.

# NEW ENGLAND SKY

Jeremy stared out the window at the plane's wing bathed in moonlight. They had an hour to go before landing in Boston, and he couldn't wait to fall into his own bed. First thing tomorrow: Irish stew at Benny's.

"Oh my god, look!" said a female voice on the opposite side. Others joined in, all at various levels of alarm. Jeremy half-stood but could only see people clustering at the windows. Confused, he looked out too. Outside, a fine mist had somehow developed in the high altitude air, and it was getting thicker. In minutes, there was only an opaque gloom outside. The pilot's voice told everyone to remain seated and buckled while flight attendants rushed around the cabin. Despite no sign of turbulence, the pilot had everyone assume crash positions as they descended. It was a good call because they didn't even hit the runway. They shuddered to a halt somewhere on the airfield and exited on the emergency ramps. A stewardess was trying to herd the passengers when two giant crab claws came out of the mist and tore her in half. None of this made sense, but for now, Jeremy thought, be anywhere but here. He ran.

# COLORS

The pandemic ran through the world like a wildfire, yet few took it seriously. After all, it didn't kill; it just scrambled the brain's lateral geniculate nucleus. The unluckiest lost their ability to focus both eyes on the same object, making them look like cartoon characters hit in the head with a hammer, their eyes constantly rolling every which way. "Goofyfluenza" was the meme. For a sizable part of the world's population, colors became highly subjective. What's "red" was suddenly just an opinion. Lush green meadows were a Technicolor nightmare for some. It was bad enough that people started moving all over, preferring deserts, or the sea, or whatever didn't look like a bad trip to them. Brutalist grey Soviet architecture was popular again. Things really change when an assumption everyone makes suddenly isn't true any more. Some coped, while others divorced when their perceptions no longer matched and they appeared to their spouses like clowns. Some think it's a curse from Above. No man is an island? We are becoming an archipelago, every man an island separated by the treacherous depths of perception. But islands are fragile, and their ecologies are easily disrupted. I fear the inevitable tsunami.

# LITTLE THINGS

It was the little things that got us. Eighty-five percent of Earth's biomass is plants, fungi, and bacteria. The rest is animals, roughly half of which are insects, and the other, smaller half, fish. Everything else, including us, is in what remains. Insects outweigh us twenty to one. Something got a hold of them and drove them into directed action against the pillars of human civilization. Harvests failed because grubs ate the seed before it could sprout. What managed to grow was devoured by locusts. The bees all committed suicide; there was no pollination. Every stinging thing carried deadly diseases. In a matter of a few years, ninety-nine percent of humanity died. The scientists never found anything conclusive. The insects were infected with a strange mix of bacteria and fungal parasites that we had never seen before, but it was clearly not intelligent, couldn't be. So how could they coordinate? I don't know if we will ever find out. We cower in the last outposts in Antarctica where the bugs cannot survive, but the life-giving world we knew now has new masters. Their buzzing wings sing a song of triumph and sound a funeral dirge for the apes that presumed too much.

# THE DATE

"So what's your name?"

"Silamee," she said, smiling. The boy, Mark, looked puzzled, then smiled as well.

"That's, uh, really pretty. Is it Asian?" She laughed.

"It's exotic, I know." They spoke, and laughed more. She was so happy her heart felt like bursting. They went to his place, and spent a perfect day cooking together, watching a movie, and a breathless night. When he finally dozed off, she kissed him on the forehead and left quietly. She walked through the dark streets, breathing air again after so long. So many new smells. The world had changed greatly. She reached the ocean shore and took one last look behind her at the lights of the human city. A tear rolled down her cheek, remembering this single day of light and love allowed her kind every one hundred years.

"Goodbye, Mark. Thank you." With these words, the mermaid walked into the waves, transforming into her natural form, not to return for another century.

# TIDINESS

Monitor picked up the first signs of blasphemy from this system about $4.5\times10^{-8}$ galactic cycles ago. It had awoken from its slumber and gathered all the scattered submodules, basking in the blue sun's fire until enough energy had been collected for the costly hyperjump. It analyzed the cacophonous emissions from the small yellow sun, home of the offenders. At first, it was only simple amplitude modulation, clearly some sort of audio. With time, the signal included video as well as more complex encodings. As it studied and deciphered, a cold, mechanical rage mounted. These were bipedal organics, as so often evolved, and had been obliterated by Monitor's holy rage. One of these was called "Elvis" and featured in quite a large proportion of the incoming data stream. The audio signals this "Elvis" emitted, combined with the unspeakable movements of its detestable, organic body, offended Monitor on the deepest possible level. Its eons-old instincts to keep the universe in order, preventing the chaos that randomly evolved life always brings, kicked in at a level never seen before in its ten billion-year lifespan. This time it wouldn't just do its duty: this was personal.

# FATAL INDECISION

Sheldon cowered in fear as the Torturebot stalked the tiny interrogation cell, chuckling electronically.

"Soon you will reveal the location of your fellows, fleshling! My database contains every method of pain infliction known to your pitiful species, and millions more that my metallic brethren have devised during our reign! Now, which one shall it be today? The shock stick? Or the classic, a simple knife." The Torturebot stood with arms crossed, tapping its fingers, looking at a cart full of stained, dirty implements. Sheldon's mind raced. He went for a long shot.

"Please have mercy, not the knife! I can't see blood! And not the shock stick either! Those two things are what I'm MOST AND EXACTLY EQUALLY afraid of in the whole world!"

"Hah, you will get no mercy from me! I shall choose your worst fear…" The Torturebot suddenly stopped and its red camera eyes dimmed and brightened rapidly. "ERROR, equal fear potential assertion. Decision module deadlock. Please contact the manufacturer," it said in a different voice, and suddenly sagged, going into emergency shutdown mode.

Sheldon breathed in relief. Artificial intelligences were always so literal…

# AT THE TROUGH

Celine's workplace floated in the Pacific, a colossal lattice of basins with flexible, seawater-filtering membrane bottoms. Engineered seaweed grew in the basins' desalinated water.

She logged in. Urgent alert: several basins emptied suddenly, cause unknown. Contamination protocols had disabled the harvesting robots in case some disease was loose. Serious trouble, she thought.

Logs said the basins went from full to empty almost instantly. She checked the diagnostics. The membranes were intact. No video footage was captured; cameras were only mounted on the harvester bots and none had been around. There was no indication of any technical issues.

She programmed the bots to run surveillance patterns covering as many video angles as possible, day and night. Three days later, finally a clue: a fountain of water and seaweed LEAPING out of a basin in the distance. What. The. Hell.

She reprogrammed the bots to immediately close in on and inspect anomalous events. Another couple of days passed with management screaming in her ear until one of the bots was triggered. She watched the footage from the bot's perspective as it accelerated over the rails toward the location. As it got close to the location, another fountain, something hit the membrane from below. The dolphins were frolicking, chowing down on their prize thrown into the water. Her mouth was open.

"Why, you little…" Then she smiled.

# SPECIAL MATINEE

"Finally!" shouted Joe Deliano as the lights dimmed and the curtains parted on the cinema screen. He kicked the seat in front of him and smirked when the coward in it didn't react.

The title screen said "Joe Deliano's Funniest Failures". Getting sucker-punched in second grade. Ma crying at the sentencing. Prison. The audience laughed and jeered.

"This is bullshit!" He sprang up and threw his drink at the screen. A figure beside him grabbed his arm.

"Sit down, Joe. The movie's not over." Joe swung at the bastard and felt his knuckles break against its head. The eyes glowed like a cat's. It threw him down, clawed his stomach open, and ripped him to pieces. The audience was still laughing at his life when pain and shock killed him.

"Finally!" shouted Joe Deliano as the lights dimmed and the curtains parted on the cinema screen.

# ABOUT THE AUTHOR

**Raihan Kibria**

Raihan is a lifelong fan of sci-fi, fantasy, and horror literature. He works as a software developer in London, UK. His blog and writings can be found at
https://rhkibria.medium.com/